ORDER OF BLACKWING

Laura Shenton

ORDER OF BLACKWING

Laura Shenton

Iridescent Toad Publishing

Chapter One

A golden sunbeam pierced the dawn mist, casting a warm, ethereal glow upon the elven kingdom of Tunildia. Shaniah stepped out of her cosy cottage – a generous gift from the king. Her eyes, an unusual blend of gold and stormy grey, shimmered with anticipation. Today was her twenty-first birthday – a day she had been eagerly awaiting.

As she began her journey to the training grounds, Shaniah's striking features caught the morning light. Her delicate elven ears occasionally peeked through her long dark hair that flowed like a river at midnight. Her slender yet athletic build, honed through rigorous training sessions, moved with purpose as she navigated the quiet streets.

The cobblestones glistened with dew beneath her feet as she made her way through the town. She inhaled deeply, savouring the cool, damp air that carried the scent of rich earth and blossoming flowers. The picturesque landscape seemed to celebrate alongside her, the vibrant colours of the kingdom's flora painted by the still-rising sun.

"Ah, if it isn't the half-breed," a sneering voice rang out, shattering the peaceful moment.

Much to Shaniah's contempt, Kei emerged from the shadows, his angular face twisted in disdain. His icy blue eyes belied his frigid demeanour, and his auburn hair was tied back tightly in a bun that didn't quite flatter him. He was flanked by his companions Yana and Albia.

Shaniah's grip tightened on the strap of her bag as she fought to control her annoyance. Amongst the full-blooded elves, known for their dedication to old magical traditions, some viewed her mixed heritage and lack of magic as a blemish upon their pristine society. Kei, in particular, never missed an opportunity to taunt her. The constant disrespect and alienation she faced from some of the locals in Tunildia due to her half-breed status had always been a sore point for Shaniah, fuelling a deep-seated anger at the injustice of it all.

"Leave me be, Kei," Shaniah said, her voice wavering between defiance and vulnerability. "I have no time for your games."

"Is that how you speak to your betters?" Kei drawled as he flicked open a dagger with practiced ease, carrying himself with an air of arrogance as he advanced. "Perhaps I should teach you some respect."

"Enough!" a female voice commanded.

Wygia – the king's daughter – strode towards them, her silver hair glinting in the sunlight. She possessed an ethereal beauty characteristic of elves. Her green eyes reflected both wisdom and determination, and she carried herself with grace and poise, yet there was an undeniable strength in her lithe form. She glared at Kei, a silent challenge.

"Princess Wygia," Kei said with false deference, bowing as he sheathed his dagger. "I meant no disrespect."

"Your actions say otherwise," Wygia countered sharply. "Be off with you."

With a final glare at Shaniah, Kei and his companions retreated, leaving her alone with the princess. Shaniah's gaze lingered on her saviour for a moment before she too turned away, her heart heavy with an odd mixture of gratitude and frustration. As much as she appreciated Wygia's intervention, she resented the constant reminder that she couldn't stand up to her tormentors on her own.

"Happy birthday, Shaniah," Wygia said softly, a gentle smile decorating her pretty features.

"Thanks for the rescue, but I don't need your help," Shaniah snapped, her voice strained with guilt.

She just couldn't shake the feeling that in accepting Wygia's assistance, she was admitting her own weakness.

"Shaniah, it wasn't about help. It was about doing what's right," Wygia replied evenly, unfazed by Shaniah's anger. "Now, we can either stand here bickering, or make good use of our time."

As much as Shaniah didn't want to admit it, Wygia had a point. Clenching her jaw, she followed the princess. They walked together past timber-framed houses until the town faded behind them. The landscape shifted to rolling meadows and ancient oak trees, the air growing cooler and tinged with the scent of pine. Ahead, the training grounds lay nestled in a tranquil glade, awaiting their arrival.

Upon reaching the sparring ring delineated by a circle of finely crushed gravel, Wygia drew her practice sword.

"Defensive stance," she ordered.

Shaniah mirrored the action, gripping her own wooden weapon tightly, her knuckles turning white.

"Let's see how well you can hold your ground," Wygia challenged.

With a nod, Shaniah braced herself for the first blow. Wygia struck swiftly, her movements fluid and precise. Shaniah parried the attack, her muscles tensing as she anticipated the next strike. Anger fuelled her focus, narrowing her world down to the dance between their practice swords.

"Your anger is driving you, Shaniah," Wygia observed, her voice steady and authoritative, even as their blades clashed, "but it also clouds your judgment."

Sometimes, anger is what keeps me going, Shaniah thought bitterly.

She blocked another blow from Wygia, her breaths coming in short, ragged pants.

"Anger can be powerful, but it's also unpredictable," Wygia continued, pressing her advantage. "You need to find balance, Shaniah. Only then can you truly excel."

"That's easy for you to say," Shaniah retorted.

She gritted her teeth as she deflected another of Wygia's attacks. Feeling a pang of humiliation at being lectured mid-duel, her frustration only intensified.

"Enough talking," Shaniah muttered under her breath.

She lunged forward in an attempt to seize control of the duel, but in her haste, she left herself open. In a swift, fluid movement, Wygia sidestepped the attack and disarmed Shaniah with a flick of her wrist. The practice sword soared through the air, landing with a thud several feet away. Shaniah stood there, weaponless, as the reality of the situation washed over her like an icy wave.

"Take this lesson to heart," Wygia advised. "There will always be those who seek to provoke you, but it's up to you how you choose to respond. In every battle, remember that your greatest enemy is often yourself."

As Shaniah stared into Wygia's unwavering gaze, she couldn't help but recognise the truth in the princess' words. Though her pride smarted from the defeat, she knew she would have to find a way to conquer her anger and embrace the inner strength that she hoped lay buried beneath.

"Anger can be a powerful weapon," Wygia said, "but it's a double-edged one. It can destroy your enemies or consume you from within. The world will test you in ways you cannot imagine. You may soon find yourself faced with challenges that require not just raw strength, but wisdom and restraint. Your true potential lies there, waiting to be unlocked."

Shaniah winced at Wygia's cryptic words. It felt as if she was hinting at some ominous change on the horizon. Although Shaniah had spent years dreaming of discovering her true purpose, the thought of leaving the kingdom filled her with dread.

"What are you getting at?" Shaniah asked cautiously.

"I cannot say more," Wygia said, turning to look into the distance. "But know that when the time comes, you'll have to choose between the path of anger and the path of wisdom. Only one will lead to victory, and the other to ruin."

As the words hung in the air, tension coiled in Shaniah's chest. This day, her twenty-first birthday, which had once held so much promise, now seemed marred by foreboding. Yet, as she reflected on Wygia's words, a spark of hope ignited within her. Wygia had always been kind, diligently training her to be stronger. Though Shaniah couldn't quite fathom why Wygia had always shown such unwavering support, their friendship had blossomed into something deeply meaningful. In Wygia, Shaniah found courage, and in return, she offered loyalty and companionship. Over the years, they had shared countless moments of laughter and intrigue, each pushing the other to grow and thrive. Their bond was not just of mentor and student, but of equals, each drawing joy and comfort from the other's presence.

"Thank you, Wygia," Shaniah managed, swallowing the lump in her throat. "I'll keep it in mind."

"See that you do," Wygia said, her voice softening. "Now, I must attend to my duties."

With a graceful nod, Wygia departed, to the castle, Shaniah presumed. As she watched the princess walk away, Shaniah's mind drifted to King Bartolm, the ruler of Tunildia. He had always shown her such kindness. From gifting her the cottage, to his thoughtful gestures, the generosity of his actions puzzled her. She wasn't sure why he treated her with such exception, but he was a lovely man – one she looked up to, and one whose paternal guidance she was grateful for.

Shaniah took a deep breath, savouring the crisp air. Surrounded by ancient trees, the training grounds seemed to pulse with potential. As she bent to retrieve her fallen practice sword, she made a silent vow to herself. She would master her anger, unlock her true potential, and prove to everyone – including herself – that she was more than just a half-breed.

With a renewed sense of purpose, she began her solo practice, her movements growing more fluid and controlled with each passing moment. The sun climbed higher in the sky, casting dappled shadows through the leaves, as if nature itself was watching and waiting to see what the half-elven woman would become.

Chapter Two

Shaniah's slender frame was almost lost among the branches of the large tree. As she sat on a particularly sturdy one, her delicate elven ears peeked through her dark hair as she watched the stormy skies in the west. The world around her seemed to hold its breath, a rapturous beauty that stirred even the deepest corners of her soul. Yet, she couldn't fully appreciate it; her thoughts were consumed by the lands beyond Tunildia's borders, particularly the human kingdoms. She wondered if she belonged in one of them.

Many afternoons had been spent perched on this very spot, daydreaming about those distant places, so different from the serene elven kingdom where she'd lived since as long as she could remember.

As a child, Shaniah had quickly learned that she was different from the elves in Tunildia. Her physical proportions – and even her mannerisms – presented as distinctly human. She was a half-breed, an identity that marked her as an outsider among the elegant, delicate elves who surrounded her.

"Patience, Shaniah," King Bartolm had often told her, keen to soothe her worries after particularly cruel taunts from her peers. "You are not defined by their narrow-mindedness. Your spirit is stronger than their disdain."

Despite the king's reassurances, the constant scorn had always gnawed at Shaniah, deepening her sense of alienation. When she looked in the mirror, all she could see were the differences – the infuriating quirks that set her apart from the established visage of elven perfection.

Her mind drifted back to the morning's confrontation from Kei. Frustration rose like bile in her throat as she recalled his audacity, and how it had impacted her mindset for the sparring session with Wygia thereafter. Her inability to manage her temper had cost her.

"Shaniah," came a familiar voice, patient and gentle.

Shaniah turned to see Wygia sat beside her on the branch, a look of concern etched upon her flawless features.

"Don't be so hard on yourself," Wygia said, her observant expression reflecting a wisdom that belied her youthful appearance.

"That's easier said than done," Shaniah retorted. "It's ok for you. You're the embodiment of elven perfection."

"Perfection is an illusion," Wygia insisted, her tone sharpening to reveal her fierce determination. "We all have our burdens. Besides, my intention is not to flaunt my elven heritage, Shaniah. We are friends, after all."

Shaniah sighed, turning her gaze back towards the stormy horizon.

"What does it matter?" she muttered, her voice tinged with bitterness. "I don't belong here anyway. Perhaps my fate lies with the humans."

"Perhaps," Wygia allowed, her voice

softening. "Who knows where destiny will take you."

As the wind whispered a melancholy tune through the branches, Shaniah's heart ached with unanswered questions. Her focus remained fixed on the horizon, where she imagined her parents standing hand in hand, their love like an eternal flame. She longed to understand her place in the world, to embrace her dual heritage without sadness or shame. But the pain of abandonment never ceased, leaving her adrift in a sea of uncertainty.

With today being her twenty-first birthday, her questions of who her parents were – and why they had left her – had become unexpectedly magnified. It was as if the milestone had cast a spotlight on her sense of emptiness, intensifying her yearning to uncover her past. A day that should have been filled with joy and promise only served to deepen the void within. She couldn't shake the feeling that somewhere, answers awaited her, just out of reach, tantalisingly close yet exasperatingly distant.

A sudden gust of wind ripped through the tree's branches, jolting Shaniah out of her reverie. She watched as Wygia braced herself against the gale, her silver hair streaming behind her like a banner.

"Shaniah," Wygia said, her voice clear and steady despite the howling wind, "I have news that concerns you. Father would like to see you this evening – he wishes to speak about your future, among other things."

Shaniah couldn't help but feel a burgeoning curiosity; she sensed that Wygia was holding something back.

"Tell me," said Wygia, "if you could know your future – if it had already been written – would you want that knowledge?"

The question unsettled Shaniah. She hesitated, her thoughts a whirlwind of conflicting emotions.

"I... I'm not sure," she admitted, her tone edged with uncertainty. "Why do you ask?"

"Because some truths are not easy to hear," Wygia said solemnly, her eyes filled with a sorrow that seemed ancient and heavy. "And sometimes, ignorance can be a balm for the soul."

"Are you saying that what the king has to share will bring me pain?" Shaniah demanded, her concern blossoming into anger.

"Only that the road ahead may be more difficult than you imagine," Wygia answered gently, placing a reassuring hand on Shaniah's shoulder. "But you have the strength to endure, even if the path is fraught with peril."

"Enough with the riddles, Wygia!" Shaniah snapped, her patience wearing thin. "Just tell me what the king wants!"

"Only he can reveal his intentions," Wygia replied, her voice firm but compassionate. "You must meet him in the throne room later tonight."

Shaniah sensed that Wygia perhaps wished she could reveal more about what the king wanted to say. The thought was somewhat comforting. Besides, she knew that Wygia's loyalty to her father was unwavering. Shaniah respected this devotion deeply, just as she respected the king. Even though the present secrecy was maddening, she trusted that both Wygia and the king had her best interests at heart. Their actions, no matter how enigmatic, were always driven by a desire to protect and guide her. Calmed by the realisation, Shaniah took a deep breath, the anger ebbing away as she met Wygia's gaze.

"I'm sorry for snapping at you," she said, her remorse evident in her tone. "I just don't know what to expect."

"It's alright," Wygia replied with a gentle smile. "I understand. It's not every day that father is so formal about wanting to see you. Just promise me you won't sit here all afternoon getting upset and worried. You'll drive yourself mad!"

With that, Wygia jumped down from the branch. She paused momentarily to look back up at Shaniah, lifting her hand in a polite wave before darting off into the foliage.

Shaniah watched the now-peaceful spot, her heart pounding with both anticipation and dread. As the storm clouds gathered above her, she couldn't shake the feeling that her long-awaited birthday might end not in celebration, but in regret.

Chapter Three

The cool, damp earth beneath Shaniah's boots gave way to the cobbled streets of Tunildia as she left the forest path behind her. Twilight was settling over the town, its lantern-lit windows casting a warm, golden glow that bathed the ancient stone buildings in a welcoming embrace. But still Shaniah pulled her hood up in an attempt to shield herself from prying eyes.

As she navigated the winding streets, memories of childhood walks with King Bartolm flooded her mind. The thought of his strong hand firmly holding hers, guiding her through the darkened forest as they spoke of legends and lore, brought a bittersweet ache to her heart. It had been during those walks that she'd found solace and comfort.

"Come along, young Shaniah," he had told her, his voice as vibrant and regal as ever. "There's still much for you to learn, and this forest holds secrets that even I have yet to uncover."

Shaking off the feeling of nostalgia, Shaniah focused on the task at hand. After leaving the large tree earlier that day, she had spent hours wandering alone in the forest, letting the familiar surroundings calm her frayed nerves. But as evening approached and the shadows deepened, anxiety had begun to gnaw at her once more.

"Shaniah!" called Broman Cillidah, the commander of the elven army, his voice warm and welcoming.

Shaniah turned to see the imposing figure of Commander Cillidah approaching. He was a tall, broad-shouldered elf with piercing blue eyes that seemed to hold eons of wisdom. His silver hair was pulled back in a tight braid, and he wore the ornate armour of his station, adorned with intricate elven designs. Despite his intimidating appearance, his face bore a kind smile that put Shaniah at ease.

"Commander Cillidah," she greeted, pulling down her hood. "It's good to see you."

"How is your training going?" he asked. "I hear that you have been putting the hours in with Wygia."

"It's challenging, but rewarding," Shaniah admitted. "I don't always get it right, but I appreciate everything Wygia is trying to do for me."

"That's the spirit," Commander Cillidah said approvingly. "You have a bright future ahead, Shaniah. Just remember, sometimes strength comes from within, not just from the blade."

"I'll remember that," she promised.

"Good," he said with a friendly smile. "Oh, and one more thing: I have it on good authority that you might receive a gift for your coming of age – something that already belongs to you, in a sense."

"Already belongs to me?" Shaniah echoed curiously. "What could that be?"

The commander merely winked, a mysterious grin playing on his lips.

"You'll find out soon enough," he said. "Farewell, Shaniah. May the stars guide your path."

With that, he departed, leaving Shaniah with a sense of anticipation.

What does everyone seem to know that I don't? she wondered, a frustration brewing that she tried her best to ignore.

As Shaniah approached the castle, the sight of a large black bird – a raven – caused her to shudder with unease. Perched on a high wall, the raven's obsidian feathers gleamed in the fading light, its intelligent eyes fixed upon her with an unnerving intensity. Time seemed to slow as Shaniah locked eyes with the bird.

This wasn't the first time she had encountered a raven. Over the years, ravens had appeared in her dreams and waking life at pivotal moments. She remembered the raven that had watched her from a gnarled tree branch on the day she began her combat training, and another that had circled overhead when she'd first recognised her inability to perform magic. Each sighting had coincided with a significant change or revelation in her life.

In her dreams, the ravens spoke to her in cryptic whispers, their words lost upon waking but leaving behind a lingering sense of foreboding. Sometimes, she dreamed of flying with them, soaring over Tunildia and beyond, to lands she had never seen before but somehow knew.

As the bird took flight and vanished into the night sky, its wings cutting through the air with silent precision, Shaniah couldn't shake the feeling that it was an omen. The raven's appearance now, on the evening of her meeting with King Bartolm, seemed particularly significant.

Perhaps it's just my nerves, she thought, trying to dispel the apprehension that clung to her.

The warmth of the castle beckoned. Shaniah stepped inside, her silhouette forming flickering shadows on the walls. She shrugged off her cloak and hung it on a nearby peg, grateful for the respite from the cold.

On her journey through the vast castle, her footsteps echoed in the grand corridors. It was a masterpiece of elven architecture, its soaring ceilings and graceful arches a testament to the skill and artistry of its builders. As she walked, Shaniah marvelled at the intricate tapestries that adorned the walls, depicting scenes from elven history and mythology.

She passed through a great hall where ornate chandeliers cast a warm glow over the polished marble floors. The light danced off suits of armour standing at attention along the walls, their craftsmanship evident in every curve and detail. Shaniah's fingers trailed along the cool stone of a pillar as she ascended a sweeping staircase, its steps worn smooth by centuries of use.

The upper floors of the castle were no less impressive. Shaniah walked through corridors lined with portraits of past elven rulers, their eyes seeming to follow her as she passed. Moonlight streamed through the stained glass windows, projecting muted yet colourful patterns on the floor and walls, a homage to scenes of elven lore that Shaniah had heard in bedtime stories as a child.

Finally, she reached one of her favourite rooms in the castle: the kitchen. As she turned to peer inside, she spotted Kimdah, her heart swelling with affection at the sight of the elven woman who had been like a mother to her.

Kimdah was a vision of grace and wisdom, her endearing pudginess adding to her pleasant aura. Her hair, a shimmering silver, was intricately braided and adorned with small sparkling gems. Her expressive face bore the subtle lines of laughter and kindness, and her eyes, a deep violet, held an abundance of knowledge. She wore flowing robes of midnight blue, embroidered with constellations in silver thread.

"Shaniah, my dear," Kimdah said, opening her arms wide. "You've arrived just in time for dinner."

"Kimdah," Shaniah enthused as she stepped into the embrace, the nostalgic scent of lavender and sage enveloping her. "I'm glad to see you."

"Come," said Kimdah, taking Shaniah's hand and guiding her towards the dining hall. "Let's eat."

As they sat down to a steaming meal of roasted vegetables and tender venison, Shaniah couldn't help but think of her upcoming meeting with King Bartolm. She chewed thoughtfully, savouring the rich flavours while her mind raced.

"Kimdah, do you know why King Bartolm wishes to speak with me tonight?" she asked hesitantly, hoping for some insight.

"Ah, my child," Kimdah replied gently. "I cannot say for certain, but I assure you, the king has always held you in high regard. Listen to his wisdom, and trust that he has your best interests at heart."

Although Kimdah's presence was soothing, Shaniah couldn't quell her anxiety. She looked down at her plate and fiddled with a stray strand of hair.

"Shaniah," Kimdah said softly, sensing her unease. "Don't underestimate your ability to handle whatever life throws at you. You are strong and capable. Trust in yourself."

"Thank you, Kimdah," Shaniah said quietly, touched by the kind words, but still worried about the potential revelations awaiting her.

"Now, eat up," Kimdah said enthusiastically, trying to lift the mood. "The king will be expecting you soon."

***

After dinner, Shaniah retreated to her chamber to change into formal attire. This place, nestled within the heart of the castle, brought a small measure of comfort in its familiarity. Growing up in the castle under King Bartolm's generous hospitality, Shaniah had spent most of her childhood within its walls. Even after being gifted her cottage by the king, the castle still felt like home to her.

Her hands shook with nervous anticipation as she donned a flowing gown of deep emerald, the colour complementing her pale skin. She stared at her reflection, barely recognising the woman looking back at her, a blend of fragility and stoicism etched across her face. The restless feeling clawing at her insides threatened to overwhelm her, but she refused to let it win.

As she walked down the hallway towards the throne room, Shaniah's thoughts returned to her childhood walks with King Bartolm.

Those moments of respite from the world's judgment and her own self-doubt were precious memories that she clung to like a lifeline. The king had been more than just a ruler; he had been a mentor, a friend, and a father figure. Would tonight's revelations change their bond forever?

Chapter Four

As she stood outside the looming oak doors of the throne room, anxiety coiled within Shaniah like a viper, tightening its grip. The weight of anticipation pressed down on her, making each breath a conscious effort.

Get a hold of yourself, she thought.

She clenched her fist around her prayer bracelet, the cool metal offering a small comfort against the storm raging within her. The intricate patterns carved into each bead whispered stories of love, loss, and faith.

Knowing that she couldn't delay the inevitable, with a deep breath, Shaniah summoned her courage and pushed open the large doors. They swung inward with a soft groan, revealing the majestic throne room.

Despite having been in the throne room many

times before, the sheer grandeur of it never failed to impress Shaniah. Vaulted ceilings soared above her, adorned with frescoes that chronicled the proud history of Tunildia. Gleaming chandeliers cast a warm, golden glow across the polished marble floors, their light illuminating the intricate tapestries lining the walls.

At the far end of the hall sat King Bartolm upon his throne. Even from a distance, his regal bearing commanded attention. As Shaniah approached, she took in the details of his appearance. His silver hair, streaked with strands of pure white, was bound by a circlet of gold adorned with emeralds that matched his piercing green eyes. His face, though lined with the wisdom of years, still held a youthful vigour. He wore robes of deep crimson and gold, and upon his chest rested an amulet that seemed to pulse with an inner vibrance.

Wygia stood quietly by his side, her presence not merely supportive, but active and vigilant, reflecting her deep involvement in what was about to unfold.

Their combined presence, though imposing, offered a paradoxical comfort. The grandeur of the king and the quiet strength of Wygia anchored Shaniah amidst her swirling vortex of uncertainty. Knowing they cared deeply for her provided a small measure of reassurance as she faced the unknown, even if it did little to ease her worries overall.

"Welcome, Shaniah," King Bartolm announced, his voice rich and resonant, filling the large room as he offered her a genuine smile.

Shaniah dropped into a deep curtsy, her emerald gown pooling around her feet.

"Your Majesty," she replied, her voice steady despite her racing nerves.

As she rose, the king's piercing gaze locked onto hers, as if assessing her readiness for the gravity of what was about to be revealed. A moment of silence stretched between them, thick with anticipation.

"Come closer, child," King Bartolm said at last, gesturing to a beautifully carved chair that had been placed before the dais. "What I have to tell you is deeply important."

Shaniah approached, her footsteps echoing in the vast space. As she settled into the chair, she noticed the king exchanging a meaningful glance with Wygia.

"Shaniah," he began, his tone gentler now, "you have grown into a remarkable young woman. Your strength, your determination, your kindness: they are all wonderful qualities, none of which have gone unnoticed."

"Thank you, Your Majesty," Shaniah murmured, a blend of pride and confusion swelling within her and making her wonder what the conversation would lead to.

"There is a reason why I have always taken a special interest in your wellbeing," King Bartolm said as he leaned forward. "A reason why I gifted you that cottage, why I've ensured you received the best upbringing and opportunities."

Shaniah's heart began to race. She had always wondered about the king's generosity towards her – a half-breed in a kingdom of pure-blooded elves. Deep down, she had often questioned if his kindness was driven by pity. After all, he was a wonderfully generous man with a deep sense of compassion.

"Your Majesty," she said. "I appreciate everything you have done for me."

"The pleasure is all mine, but the reason runs deeper than you think," said the king, a hint of sorrow creeping into his expression as he breathed a heavy sigh. "Shaniah, you are more than just a deserving subject of my kingdom. You are family."

Shaniah's breath caught in her throat.

"Family?" she repeated, her mind reeling.

"Yes," King Bartolm confirmed, nodding solemnly. "Many years ago, I had a younger sister named Nheve. Tragically, her life was cut short – she was murdered."

Shaniah gasped, her hand flying to her mouth in shock. Her thoughts raced, trying to process this new information. How could she have never known that the king had a sister? And what terrible circumstances could have led to her demise?

"Your Majesty, I... I had no idea," she said, her voice trembling with emotion at the thought of the pain he must have endured.

"Few in Tunildia know of her story," the king

admitted, a far-off look in his eyes. "Nheve was a beacon of hope, ahead of her time. She married King Vygor, a human. Their union was the first of its kind."

Shaniah listened intently, her heart aching at the tale of two lovers who had dared to defy convention.

"Unfortunately," King Bartolm continued, his voice holding a bitter edge, "their dream of unity died with them. The kingdom they ruled together, Blackwing, fell into darkness after their deaths. It is now a shadow of its former glory, a land shrouded in despair."

Shaniah winced as she tried to make sense of this revelation. The story of Nheve and Vygor, though tragic, felt strangely close to her own struggles for acceptance and understanding.

"But why are you telling me this now?" she asked.

The king took a deep breath, as if steeling himself for what he was about to say next.

"Because, Shaniah, this story is not just a piece of forgotten history. It is *your* history."

Shaniah's eyes widened as she gripped the arms of her chair.

"Your full name," he said, pausing as if to ensure she was ready to hear what was to come, "is Shaniah Blackwing. You are the daughter of King Vygor and my sister, Queen Nheve."

The revelation struck Shaniah like a bolt of lightning. The shock of it made her stand up reflexively, as if her emotion demanded a physical response.

"I... I'm a princess?" she stammered, the words feeling foreign on her tongue.

"Yes," King Bartolm confirmed. "You are the rightful heir to the throne of Blackwing."

Shaniah felt as though the world was tilting beneath her feet. The king's voice seemed to come from far away as he continued speaking.

"Blackwing, the kingdom your parents once ruled, now suffers under the cruel reign of a tyrannical queen," he said. "It is time for you to claim your birthright, Shaniah – to challenge the darkness that threatens your people and restore balance to your homeland."

Shaniah's pulse roared in her ears, drowning out all other sounds as she grappled with the enormity of her newfound heritage. For the first time, she now knew the identities of her parents – if only by name and the tragic circumstances of their deaths. This revelation was more than mere information; it was a profound moment of validation and connection. After years of wondering and unanswered questions, these names were a key to unlocking her past. It was as though she was standing on the brink of a new reality that had always been just beyond her grasp.

"Your Majesty," she said shakily, "I don't know what to do. How can I possibly face this when I've only just learned the truth?"

"You have the strength within you, Shaniah," King Bartolm replied, his words resolute but compassionate. "The same strength that your mother possessed. You are not alone in this fight. We will stand by you."

It was all too much for Shaniah to bear. Her vision blurred. The opulent throne room seemed to spin and swirl around her like a whirlpool. She could no longer feel the floor beneath her feet. With a shuddering breath, she collapsed into unconsciousness.

Chapter Five

Shaniah lay motionless on her bed, absently focused on the stone ceiling of her chamber as the last rays of sunset filtered through the window. For two days, she had remained here, a self-imposed exile from the world that had suddenly become foreign to her.

The weight of her newfound reality pressed down upon her, leaving her struggling to comprehend the events that had unfolded. 'Coming of age' had taken on a different connotation, one she could hardly bear to think about. No longer was it simply a celebration of adulthood; now, it signified her responsibility to ascend a throne she wasn't even sure she wanted or deserved.

During her seclusion, King Bartolm, Wygia, and Kimdah had all attempted to coax her out, each in their own kind and patient ways.

Their gentle knocks on the chamber door and softly-spoken words had gone unanswered. Shaniah couldn't bring herself to face them, not when the hurt of their deception still stung so sharply.

How could they have kept this from her? All these years, she had endured taunts and sidelong glances, never understanding why she was different. Half-elf, half-human – a curiosity in a kingdom of pure-blooded elves. And all along, they had known. King Bartolm, Wygia, Kimdah, even Commander Cillidah – they had all been privy to a secret that could have eased her pain, given her a sense of understanding, a sense of identity.

As night fell, Shaniah drifted into an uneasy sleep, where reality blurred and the impossible became tangible.

In her dream, she found herself standing in a vast meadow, the likes of which she had never seen in Tunildia. The grass beneath her bare feet was cool and damp, each blade a vibrant green that seemed to pulse with life. A gentle breeze caressed her skin, carrying with it the intoxicating scent of wildflowers – delicate lavender, sweet honeysuckle, and the earthy aroma of chamomile. She inhaled deeply, embracing the fragrant air. It was a scent that spoke of freedom, of untamed wilderness. For a moment, Shaniah felt a sense of belonging she had never experienced before.

As she took a step forward, the soft earth yielded beneath her toes. The meadow seemed to stretch endlessly in all directions, a sea of gently waving grass. But then, something in the distance caught her attention: a shimmering pool of water that seemed to call to her.

Drawn by an unseen force, Shaniah approached the pool. Its surface was as still as glass, reflecting the azure sky above with perfect clarity. She knelt at its edge, curious as she leaned forward to observe her reflection.

At first, she saw herself as she always had – a familiar blend of elven and human features that had marked her as different her entire life. But as she watched, the image began to change. Her reflection rippled and distorted, as if the water itself was alive and writhing beneath the surface.

Horror gripped Shaniah as her reflection transformed. Her eyes, once a unique blend of gold and stormy grey, now glowed with an otherworldly light. Her skin took on a pallid hue, stretched taut over sharpened cheekbones. Her lips, usually soft and full, thinned and curved into a cruel smile that sent shivers down her spine.

Shaniah tried to recoil from the nightmarish vision, but found herself frozen in place, unable to look away from this twisted version of herself. A feeling of panic rose in her throat, but there was nothing she could do to get away from the harrowing sight before her.

Just as she felt she might be lost to the terror, a weight settled on her left shoulder. Startled, she tore her focus from the pool to find a raven had settled upon her, its feathers so black they seemed to absorb the very light around them.

Although the bird's presence should have frightened her further, Shaniah felt an inexplicable sense of calm wash over her. Its beady eyes, dark as onyx, met hers with an intelligence that seemed almost human. There was a wisdom, and something else – a hint of shared secrets and untold stories.

With the raven's talons gently gripping her shoulder, Shaniah felt anchored to reality in a way she hadn't before. The surreal landscape of the dream, which had threatened to sweep her away in its strangeness, now felt more manageable. The raven's presence, though undeniably foreboding, offered an odd comfort that she couldn't quite explain.

Shaniah raised a tentative hand, her fingers hovering near the raven's midnight plumage. The bird made no attempt to retreat, instead cocking its head slightly as if in curiosity. As her fingertips brushed against its feathers, softer than she had imagined, a jolt of energy coursed through her body.

Images flashed before her eyes: a dense forest engulfed in shadows, a tarnished crown lying forgotten in a field of ashes, a sword gleaming with an inner fire. Each vision vanished almost as quickly as it had appeared, leaving Shaniah bewildered.

The raven's beak opened, and Shaniah leaned in, certain it was about to speak. Instead of words, however, she heard a sound that didn't belong in this dreamscape: a knock, sharp and insistent, echoing from somewhere beyond the meadow.

With a gasp, she found herself back in her

chamber, the last wisps of the dream clinging to her consciousness like cobwebs.

The knock came again, more urgent this time. Shaniah's attention shifted to the heavy wooden door of her chamber, her mind still caught between the dream and reality.

"Shaniah?"

It was Wygia's voice, muffled by the thick wood.

Shaniah blinked, trying to shake off the lingering effects of her dream.

"Shaniah! I need to speak with you."

Shaniah's stomach growled, reminding her that she couldn't stay locked away forever. She pushed herself up on shaky arms, her body protesting after days of inactivity. As she swung her legs over the side of the bed, her bare feet touching the cold stone floor, she couldn't help but remember the feel of soft grass beneath them in her dream.

"Fine," she said with a sigh as she approached the door.

She turned the key in the lock. The moment

she stepped away from the door, Wygia swept in, her expression a blend of concern and determination.

"What do you want?" Shaniah asked bluntly, her voice hoarse from disuse.

"Shaniah," Wygia said gently, her expression softening. "I... we've been worried about you. May I sit? I think it's time we talked properly."

After a moment's hesitation, Shaniah nodded. She perched on the edge of her bed while Wygia took a seat in a nearby chair.

"I know you're hurt," Wygia began. "And you have every right to be. We kept a tremendous secret from you – one that has caused you pain throughout your life."

"Why?" Shaniah asked, her voice cracking. "Why did you all lie to me for so long?"

"We struggled with that decision every day, Shaniah. But we believed – we still believe – that it was necessary to protect you."

"Protect me?" Shaniah scoffed. "From what? The truth?"

"From the danger that truth brings," Wygia

countered. "Imagine if you had known as a child. You might have run off to Blackwing, vulnerable and untrained. We couldn't risk losing you like that."

"So instead, you let me grow up feeling like an outsider?" Shaniah probed, anger rising in her voice. "Do you have any idea what it's like to never understand why you're different, why people look at you with disgust and pity?"

"You're right," Wygia admitted, pain evident in her tone. "It's possible that we underestimated just how much that would hurt you. And for that, I am truly sorry."

Shaniah's anger deflated slightly at Wygia's sincerity.

"I just... I don't understand," she said.

"We always knew this day would come," Wygia explained. "I've trained you not just to defend yourself here in Tunildia, but to prepare you for the challenges you'll face in Blackwing. You have a birthright to claim, Shaniah. A throne to fight for."

"And what if I don't want to fight for it? What if I don't want any of this?"

Shaniah stood abruptly and began pacing the chamber. Wygia watched her every move.

"Shaniah…"

"No!" Shaniah interrupted, her voice firm. "I can't commit to fighting for a throne I've only just heard about. Why should I put myself in danger for a kingdom I don't even know? And how could I possibly take on an evil queen? I'm not capable of that, Wygia. I'm just… me."

Wygia rose, moving to stand before Shaniah.

"You are more capable than you know, Shaniah. Your parents' strength runs in your blood. But I understand your fear and hesitation. No one is asking you to make a decision immediately."

"I don't know if I can do this, Wygia. I don't know if I *want* to."

"For now, just take some time to process everything," Wygia offered kindly, placing a comforting hand on Shaniah's shoulder. "We'll be here when you're ready to talk more."

As Wygia turned to leave, she cast a lingering, empathetic look at Shaniah.

"Wygia," Shaniah said quickly. "I'm sorry for shouting at you. I know you would never want to hurt me."

"It's ok," Wygia said quietly. "I understand. Get some rest. We'll talk more when you're ready."

Wygia gave a dignified nod and then walked towards the door. As she reached for the handle, she hesitated for a brief moment, as though reluctant to leave. The air seemed to hold its breath, echoing the eternal bond that tied her to Shaniah.

Left in the quiet solitude of her chamber, Shaniah sat down slowly on the edge of her bed, her fingers tracing the pattern of the blanket in an effort to ground herself in the familiar textures. Taking a deep breath, she closed her eyes, attempting to calm the storm of emotions surging within her.

Chapter Six

The late morning sun shone through the castle windows. A gentle knock at Shaniah's chamber door broke the silence, causing her to hesitate. When she finally opened it, she saw Kimdah standing there, her kind face etched with concern and affection.

"My dear child," Kimdah said softly, her voice as soothing as a summer breeze. "May I come in?"

Shaniah nodded, stepping aside to let Kimdah cross the threshold. The older woman's presence filled the chamber with a comforting aura, reminiscent of countless childhood moments when she had been a source of solace for Shaniah.

"How are you feeling?" Kimdah asked, searching Shaniah's face for signs of distress.

"I'm… managing, I suppose," Shaniah answered with a sigh as she ran a hand through her dark hair. "It's all still so overwhelming."

"Of course it is, my dear," Kimdah said sympathetically, reaching out to squeeze Shaniah's hand. "Such news would unsettle even the strongest of hearts. But you are not alone in this, remember that."

"Thank you, Kimdah," said Shaniah, a ghost of a smile flickering across her face. "Your kindness means more than you know."

"You've always been strong, Shaniah. This revelation doesn't change who you are at your core. Never forget that."

Shaniah looked at Kimdah with a mixture of gratitude and affection. She thought about how lucky she was to have grown up around someone so generous and nurturing.

"Anyway," Kimdah said briskly, as if keen to move the conversation forward and not linger on anything too emotional. "I've come with a message from King Bartolm. He wishes to have lunch with you in the castle today."

Shaniah's heart quickened at the mention of

the king – her uncle, she reminded herself. The thought still felt foreign, surreal.

"Actually," she said, "I've been hoping to speak with him. I feel... ready now. There's so much we need to discuss."

"I'm glad to hear it, my dear. Shall I tell him you'll join him?"

"Yes, please. Tell him I'll be there shortly."

Kimdah left, and Shaniah turned to her wardrobe. Though she knew this wasn't a formal meeting, she felt compelled to present a strong front. The king had seen her at her most vulnerable – fainting at the news of her parents and heritage, locking herself away for days. Now, she wanted to show him that she was resilient, capable of facing this new reality.

She selected a turquoise tunic – a gift from Wygia a couple of birthdays ago. The colour, reminiscent of the clear lakes surrounding Tunildia, and its intricate silver embroidery caught the light as she moved. Paired with sleek black leggings and polished leather boots, the outfit struck a balance between casual and regal.

As she braided her hair, weaving in strands of silver thread that matched her tunic's embroidery, Shaniah's mind wandered to the decision she had been grappling with since her conversation with Wygia. The weight of her heritage, the throne of Blackwing, and the circumstances surrounding her parents' deaths had consumed her thoughts. She had spent countless hours pacing her chamber, analysing the risks and possibilities.

After a final glance in the mirror, Shaniah left her chamber and set out towards the dining hall. The castle corridors, though familiar, now seemed charged with new meaning. Every tapestry depicting Tunildia's history, every suit of armour standing sentinel, reminded her of the rich legacy she now knew she was part of. As she walked, her thoughts drifted to Blackwing. What history lay hidden there, and what role would she play in it now that she knew her true lineage?

Standing before the dining hall, Shaniah took a deep breath to calm her nerves. Then, she pushed open the heavy oak doors and stepped into the stunning room. Tall windows lined the walls, their stained glass filtering light into a myriad of colours that danced across the polished marble floor. A grand chandelier hung in the centre, its crystals catching the light and casting shimmering reflections throughout the room. The long ornate table, set with gleaming silverware and fine china, added to the hall's regal ambiance.

King Bartolm was already there, seated at the head of the table. At the sight of Shaniah, he rose, a warm smile spreading across his face.

"Shaniah, my dear," he said, his voice filled with affection and relief.

Before Shaniah could formulate a proper greeting, the king crossed the room in a few quick strides and enveloped her in a hearty embrace. The familiar scent of pine and parchment that always clung to him brought a rush of memories – bedtime stories, riding lessons, quiet conversations in his study. Despite the turmoil of recent days, Shaniah found herself melting into the hug, her earlier resolve to maintain a strong façade crumbling in the face of such genuine warmth.

As they separated, she looked up at the man who had raised her, seeing him in a new light.

Yes, he had kept secrets from her, but he had also given her a home, an education, and love when she had no one else. The realisation softened the edges of her lingering hurt and confusion.

"Uncle," she said, testing the word on her tongue. It felt strange, yet right somehow. "Thank you for inviting me to lunch."

"You're more than welcome," said the king, his eyes misting slightly at Shaniah's use of the familial term. "Come, let's sit and eat. We have much to discuss."

As they settled at the table, servants bringing in platters of fragrant dishes, Shaniah found herself relaxing. The familiar ritual of sharing a meal with the king – now her uncle – provided a sense of normalcy amidst the chaos of recent revelations.

They spoke of light matters at first – the food, the weather. Then, as the main course was cleared away, King Bartolm's expression grew more serious.

"Shaniah," he began, his voice gentle but firm. "I know you must have many questions about your parents, about Blackwing. I want you to know that I'm here to answer whatever I can."

"Thank you," Shaniah said, setting down her goblet. "There is so much I want to know, but perhaps we could start with their demise. What happened?"

"You were only five months old at the time," he said, his face clouding with old grief. "Your parents – my dear sister Nheve and your father, King Vygor – were murdered in their own castle."

The brutality shocked Shaniah to her core, causing her to exhale shakily.

"I suspect it was Queen Selia who orchestrated their deaths," he said, his voice heavy with regret, "though it has never been proven. She has ruled Blackwing ever since, which only strengthens my suspicions."

"Why haven't you done anything about it?" Shaniah asked, a hint of accusation creeping into her tone. "Why not investigate, or challenge her rule?"

King Bartolm sighed, the weight of years of difficult decisions evident in the slump of his shoulders.

"Blackwing is far from Tunildia, Shaniah. To openly investigate or challenge Queen Selia could have led to war – a war our people could ill afford. As much as it pained me, as much as I yearned for the truth and justice for your parents, I couldn't risk the safety of Tunildia."

Shaniah's initial flare of anger faded as she absorbed her uncle's words. She saw the pain in his eyes, the remorse etched in the lines of his face. For the first time, she truly grasped the complexity of the situation. It wasn't just her life that had been altered by her parents' deaths – her uncle had lost a beloved sister and had been forced to make impossible choices.

"I understand," she said softly, reaching across the table to grasp his hand. "It must have been a terrible burden to bear all these years."

The king squeezed Shaniah's hand, a sad smile touching his lips.

"It was," he confirmed. "But having you here, watching you grow into the strong, compassionate woman you've become: that has been a light in the darkness."

They sat in companionable silence for a

moment, each lost in thought. Finally, Shaniah took a deep breath, squaring her shoulders.

"Uncle, I've been thinking a lot over the past few days. About my parents, about Blackwing, about who I am and what I want to do."

"And what have you decided, my dear?" he asked, his tone gentle and unhurried, his gaze steady but not pressing.

He sat back slightly, giving Shaniah space to gather her thoughts. His posture conveyed openness and a willingness to listen without imposing his own expectations. His patience was evident, a silent promise to respect whatever decision she arrived at.

"I want to go to Blackwing," Shaniah said, her voice controlled despite the flutter of worry in her stomach. "I want to try to claim the throne that was stolen from my parents. I know it won't be easy, and I have so much to learn, but... it feels right. It feels like what I'm meant to do."

"Shaniah, my brave girl," said the king, pride blooming in his tone. "I had hoped you might come to this decision, but I wouldn't have forced it upon you. Know that you have my full support as you embark on this path."

Relief and determination flooded through Shaniah in equal measure.

"Thank you," she said. "I know I have a long road ahead of me, but knowing I have your support means everything."

"We will prepare you as best we can, my dear. You carry the strength of both your parents within you, and the bloodlines of two kingdoms. Blackwing may not know it yet, but their true queen is coming home."

The king stood, his expression softening as he opened his arms wide, inviting Shaniah into a warm embrace. She rose from her chair and moved towards him, closing the distance between them with ease. As she settled into the comfort of her uncle's arms, she felt a profound sense of purpose enveloping her.

Chapter Seven

The next day, Shaniah awoke with anticipation and trepidation churning in her stomach. Though she wasn't leaving for Blackwing immediately and still had more training ahead, the implications of the impending journey loomed large. Dressed in her sparring attire, her fingers trembled slightly as she laced up her boots. She couldn't help but wonder if she was truly ready for the path she had chosen.

The crisp morning air nipped at Shaniah's cheeks as she and Wygia made their way from the castle towards Tunildia's training grounds. The forest surrounding them was alive with the sound of birdsong and rustling leaves, nature seemingly oblivious to the enormity of Shaniah's circumstances. As they walked, Shaniah found herself studying Wygia's profile, marvelling at how she seemed to glow with an inner light, her silver hair catching the sunbeams that filtered through the canopy above.

"You're quiet this morning," Wygia observed, her green eyes flickering with concern as she glanced at Shaniah.

"I'm just thinking about everything. It still feels so surreal."

"It's understandable, Shaniah. I'll do my best for you today. I'll make sure to prepare you for the journey ahead as best as I possibly can."

As Wygia's reassuring words settled in her mind, Shaniah found a semblance of comfort in them. She took a deep breath, allowing the moment to bolster her resolve, even as an underlying uncertainty continued to shadow her determination.

When they emerged from the forest into the grassy clearing that served as Tunildia's training grounds, Shaniah felt a familiar rush of excitement. Despite her anxieties about the future, there was something she welcomed about the routine of training, the physical exertion that allowed her to momentarily forget her worries.

Even as memories of her last sparring session flooded back – the sting of defeat, how she had lost to Wygia because her mind had been elsewhere, still seething from the altercation with Kei – Shaniah willed herself to focus on what needed to be done: the training. She steeled herself, pushing thoughts of Kei and his taunts aside. This session couldn't be about petty personal grievances; it had to be about preparing for the journey ahead.

Wygia strode to the centre of the clearing, her movements fluid and graceful. She picked up two wooden practice swords.

"Are you ready?" she said seriously as she tossed one to Shaniah.

Shaniah deftly caught the sword, her fingers curling around the familiar weight of the hilt. She nodded, settling into a fighter's stance as Wygia began to circle her.

The bout was a flurry of movement, wooden blades clashing with resounding thwacks. Shaniah felt her body respond instinctively, years of training guiding her movements as she parried and struck. With a burst of speed, she feinted left before pivoting right, catching Wygia off guard and landing a solid hit on her side.

"Well done!" Wygia exclaimed, a proud smile lighting up her face. "Excellent footwork."

Shaniah allowed herself a moment of satisfaction, feeling a sense of accomplishment. However, as they reset for the second bout, she noticed a new intensity in Wygia's eyes – a clear sign that her trainer would push her to her limits, ensuring she would be fully prepared for the challenges ahead.

This time, Wygia attacked with renewed vigour, her movements so swift that Shaniah could barely keep up. Despite her best efforts, Shaniah found herself constantly on the defensive, struggling to find an opening. With a lightning-fast series of strikes, Wygia disarmed her, sending Shaniah's practice sword spinning across the grass.

Frustration bubbled up inside Shaniah, hot and fierce. She clenched her fists, tears of anguish threatening to spill.

"I'm not good enough," she muttered, her voice tight with emotion.

Wygia's expression softened as she approached Shaniah and placed a comforting hand on her shoulder.

"Shaniah, you mustn't attach so much emotion to losing a spar. It's the nature of training. We learn from our defeats as much as our victories."

Shaniah shrugged off Wygia's hand, pacing across the clearing as she struggled to contain her emotions.

"That's all very well," she burst out, "but losing a real battle could be deadly. How can I hope to defeat Queen Selia when I struggle so often in training?"

She stopped, her shoulders slumping as her doubts crashed over her.

"I want to go to Blackwing, to honour my parents and claim what's rightfully mine, but I'm not sure I can do it. I'm not a full-blooded elf. I don't have magical powers like you and the other elves of Tunildia. How can I hope to stand against a queen who's ruled for over two decades?"

Wygia remained silent, her focus on the distant horizon. Then, her expression shifted, a familiar look of determination settling over her features. When she turned back to face Shaniah, it was with a renewed energy, radiant and hopeful.

"Shaniah," she said, "what if you didn't have to face this alone?"

"What do you mean?" Shaniah asked, confusion replacing some of her earlier frustration.

"I could go with you to Blackwing."

The words hung in the air, heavy with implication. Shaniah was stunned by the enormity of what Wygia was offering.

"You... you would do that?" she stammered, hardly daring to believe it.

Wygia's smile was gentle and reassuring as she closed the distance between them, taking Shaniah's hands in her own.

"Of course I would. We're not just friends, Shaniah. We're family. Cousins. And family stands together, especially in times of great challenge."

Emotion welled in Shaniah's chest, a potent mixture of gratitude, love, and renewed hope.

"Wygia, I... I don't know what to say. Are you sure? This isn't your fight. You have responsibilities here in Tunildia."

"I've never been more certain of anything," Wygia replied, her voice firm with conviction. "My responsibility is to my family and to what's right. Helping you reclaim your throne and bring justice to Blackwing is the most important thing I could do."

"Thank you," Shaniah said, throwing her arms around Wygia and hugging her tightly. "I couldn't ask for a better friend or cousin."

As they separated, Wygia's expression turned serious once more.

"We should return to the castle and inform father of this development," she said. "He'll need to know, and there's much to prepare if we're to undertake this journey together."

Shaniah nodded, feeling a renewed sense of purpose coursing through her. As they began the walk back to the castle, she found herself standing a little taller, her steps more confident. The forest seemed different now, the colours more vibrant, the air charged with possibility. The path ahead would still be fraught with danger and uncertainty, but with Wygia by her side, she felt stronger.

Chapter Eight

As Shaniah and Wygia hurried through the castle's grand corridors, excitement and nervousness churned in Shaniah's stomach. Wygia's offer to accompany her on the perilous journey to Blackwing still felt surreal, but was a wonderful testament to the depth of their friendship and newly discovered familial bond.

They reached the ornate doors of King Bartolm's study, pausing for a moment to collect themselves. Shaniah glanced at Wygia, drawing strength, and then, with a deep breath, she raised her hand and knocked firmly on the door.

"Enter," came the king's voice from within.

As they stepped into the study, King Bartolm looked up from his desk, his expression softening at the sight of his daughter and niece.

"Shaniah, Wygia," he greeted, happy to see them. "What brings you here?"

Shaniah opened her mouth to speak, but found herself suddenly at a loss for words. How could she explain the magnitude of Wygia's offer?

Sensing Shaniah's hesitation, Wygia stepped forward.

"Father," she began, her voice clear and resolute, "I've made a decision. I wish to accompany Shaniah on her quest to Blackwing."

King Bartolm's eyebrows rose in surprise, his features briefly showing astonishment before settling into deep contemplation.

"Are you certain of this, Wygia?" he asked, his tone gentle but probing. "The journey to Blackwing will be fraught with danger. The challenges you'll face there..."

He trailed off, his unspoken concerns hanging in the air.

"I'm certain, Father," Wygia said firmly, her posture straightening as she met his gaze. "Shaniah is not just my friend, but my cousin. Her quest is just, and I believe it's my duty to stand by her side."

The king turned to address Shaniah, who had been watching the exchange with bated breath.

"And you, my dear?" he said. "How do you feel about this?"

"I'm... overwhelmed by Wygia's offer," she said, finding her voice at last. "It means more to me than I can express. But I also understand the enormity of what she's proposing. If you believe it's too great a risk, then I would never insist that she..."

The king held up a hand, gently silencing Shaniah.

"Wygia," he said, his voice tinged with stoicism and pride, "you are incredibly precious to me. I should perhaps counsel caution and urge you to reconsider such a dangerous undertaking. But as a father who loves you dearly, I cannot bring myself to stand in the way of what you feel is right. I trust in Shaniah's strength and resolve, and I believe in her destiny. If you feel that your presence will aid her on this path, then I must fully endorse your choice. Your guidance and support will be invaluable to her, and I have faith that together you will face whatever challenges lie ahead."

Relief washed over Shaniah, so palpable she felt her knees might buckle. Beside her, she could sense Wygia's posture relaxing as well.

"However," King Bartolm continued, his tone becoming more businesslike, "if you are to undertake this quest together, we must ensure you are both as prepared as possible. Wygia, you have the advantage of your elven magic, but there is always room for improvement. And Shaniah, while you may not possess magical abilities, understanding the nature of the power you'll be fighting alongside could prove invaluable."

As Shaniah and Wygia exchanged curious glances, the king nodded his head as if having reached a decision.

"I believe the best course of action would be for both of you to train with Commander Broman Cillidah," he said. "His expertise in both magical and physical combat will be essential in preparing you for what lies ahead."

Chapter Nine

The next morning dawned bright and clear, the air crisp with promise. Shaniah and Wygia walked together towards the training grounds. As they approached the open expanse of field, their attention was drawn to the figure waiting for them.

Commander Cillidah stood tall and confident at the centre of the space. His broad shoulders and imposing stance were matched by a presence that seemed to blend strength with wisdom. His piercing blue eyes scanned the horizon with an intensity that spoke of countless battles fought and lessons learned. The sun caught the gleam of his armour, highlighting the intricate patterns engraved on the chestplate. His expression was one of calm assurance, as though he was already evaluating the readiness of his trainees.

"Princess Wygia, Princess Shaniah," he greeted them with a respectful nod. "His Majesty has informed me of your upcoming journey. We have much work to do."

"Thank you for taking the time to support us, Commander," said Shaniah. "I appreciate it tremendously."

"You're more than welcome," he said. "I have watched you grow into a strong young woman, Shaniah. You have every right to fight for your throne in Blackwing. You have my full support."

He then turned to address Wygia, who gave a polite smile.

"Wygia, I will be working closely with you on your magic. We need to refine your control and enhance your abilities to ensure you're at your most effective."

As the training session began, Shaniah moved to the edge of the clearing and sought a spot beneath a broad tree. Though she wanted to keep a reasonable distance from the magical elements of the training, she knew it was essential to observe closely; this spot offered the perfect vantage point. From here, she had a clear view of Wygia and Commander

Cillidah as they prepared for their magical exercises. She settled down on the grass, still slightly damp with the morning dew, and made herself comfortable against the sturdy trunk. A gentle breeze rustled through the leaves, carrying the fresh scent of pine and wildflowers.

Shaniah watched, transfixed, as Wygia closed her eyes, her slender form becoming still as a statue. When her eyes fluttered open again, they glowed with an otherworldly light. The air seemed to thicken, charged with an invisible energy that made the hairs on Shaniah's arms stand on end.

With a fluid motion of her hands, Wygia conjured a shimmering barrier. It rippled like water caught in sunlight, translucent yet clearly impenetrable. Shaniah gasped, marvelling at the beauty and power of the magical shield. She had seen Wygia perform magic before, of course, but never with such intensity and purpose.

Commander Cillidah nodded approvingly, his expression tightening with concentration. He raised his hand, palm outward, and a ball of crackling energy formed at his fingertips. With a sharp gesture, he hurled it towards

Wygia's barrier. Upon impact, the magical projectile exploded in a shower of sparks, leaving the shimmering shield intact but visibly weakened.

Wygia's face was a mask of determination as she retaliated. Her fingers danced through the air, weaving intricate patterns that left trails of light in their wake. Suddenly, bolts of radiant energy shot forth from her hands, arcing through the air towards the commander. He countered with a swift series of defensive spells, deflecting some bolts and absorbing others into a swirling vortex of magic that hovered before him.

The display was nothing short of breathtaking. Shaniah found herself leaning forward, utterly captivated by the duel unfolding before her. As she watched Wygia move with fluid grace, her silver hair streaming behind her like a banner, Shaniah felt a swell of pride and affection. Wygia's face was alight with concentration and exhilaration, her every decision precise and logical. Each gesture and every incantation reflected her innate ability.

Rather than feeling intimidated or out of her depth in the face of such awe-inspiring power, Shaniah found herself filled with a profound sense of wonder and gratitude. She was fascinated by the intricate dance of magic before her, the way Wygia and Commander Cillidah wove spells as easily as others might breathe. It was beautiful, terrifying, and utterly mesmerising.

As Wygia deflected a particularly powerful spell from the commander, sending it spiralling harmlessly into the sky where it exploded in a shower of golden sparks, Shaniah felt a surge of confidence coursing through her. This was her ally, her friend, her cousin. This formidable wielder of magic would be by her side on the journey to Blackwing. The prospect of having Wygia's raw power and magical prowess complementing her own skills made the thought of the journey ahead seem less daunting.

Shaniah found herself imagining how Wygia's abilities could be applied to their upcoming quest. Her protective barriers could shield them from danger, and her offensive spells could clear a path through the obstacles they might encounter. Meanwhile, Shaniah would be ready with her blade, prepared to confront any threats that magic alone couldn't overcome.

As Wygia and Commander Cillidah paused, their voices lowering to discuss some intricate aspect of magical theory beyond Shaniah's comprehension, something else caught her attention. She turned her head and glanced up, her focus drawn to a cluster of gnarled branches above.

There, perched on a sturdy branch not more than thirty feet away, sat a raven. Its feathers gleamed in the sunlight, an iridescent sheen of blue-black that seemed almost unnatural in its perfection. Shaniah felt her breath catch in her throat, a shiver running down her spine as if a cold finger had traced her vertebrae. She couldn't help but wonder if this raven was the same one she had glimpsed outside the castle on the evening of her twenty-first birthday, or indeed the one that had appeared in her dream the other night. The resemblance was striking, yet the uncertainty made her pulse quicken as she stared at the bird, trying to decipher its significance.

The raven's presence wasn't entirely unwelcome – there was a strange beauty to the creature, after all – but it stirred a deep unease within Shaniah. Ravens had always appeared at pivotal moments in her life, silent harbingers of change and upheaval. However, what troubled her now was the growing frequency of these sightings.

Now, as she stood on the precipice of the greatest challenge of her life, preparing for a journey that would shape not only her future but the fate of an entire kingdom, Shaniah was yet again accompanied by a raven. The timing couldn't be coincidence, she thought, her heart racing. The raven's presence alongside the awe-inspiring display of elven magic – abilities she would soon rely on but could never possess – felt suspiciously meaningful.

The raven remained perfectly still, its presence a stark contrast to the dynamic energy of the magical training session. Though it made no sound, uttered no caw or cry, Shaniah couldn't shake the feeling that it was trying to communicate something of vital importance. Its silence seemed more pointed, more deliberate than mere animal behaviour.

Mesmerised, she found herself unable to look away from the bird's obsidian eyes. They were depthless pools of midnight, seeming to hold secrets and whispers of a destiny yet to unfold. Shaniah felt as though she was teetering on the edge of some great revelation, the knowledge just beyond her grasp, but tantalisingly close.

Questions raced through her mind, each one chasing the tail of the last in a dizzying whirl. Was this a sign? A portent of things to come on their perilous journey to Blackwing? Or was it a warning – a silent caution against the dangers that lay ahead? Perhaps it was a promise – a pledge from some unseen force that her chosen path, though difficult, was the right one. The raven's presence evoked both fear and exhilaration within her; it could be heralding a momentous change, whether for better or worse.

The longer Shaniah stared into those fathomless eyes, the more she felt herself slipping into a trance-like state. The sound of the training grounds – the conversation between Wygia and Commander Cillidah, the rustle of leaves in the breeze, even her own breathing – seemed to fade away. All that existed was her and the raven, locked in a silent communion that transcended ordinary understanding.

As if spellbound, Shaniah kept her gaze on the bird, her mind consumed by the enigmatic visitor.

Chapter Ten

The sun hung low on the horizon, casting shadows across the dusty path as Shaniah and Wygia trudged onward, their feet aching from days of travel. The weight of their blades, gifts from King Bartolm, served as a constant reminder of the emotional farewell they had bid to Tunildia. Shaniah's muscles still burned from the intensive training she had undergone with the elven army, while Wygia's fingers had a slight glow of residual energy from her magical sessions with Commander Cillidah.

As they walked side by side, the silence between them was comfortable. Yet, as the empty road stretched before them, seemingly endless and devoid of other travellers, Shaniah couldn't help but voice the observation that had been nagging at her.

"Have you noticed, Wygia?" she said, her voice a little croaky from disuse and the dust rising from the path as they walked. "We haven't seen another soul since we left Tunildia. Not a single traveller or merchant caravan."

"I've been thinking the same thing," said Wygia, her silver hair catching the fading sunlight as she nodded her head. "It's as if the kingdoms exist in isolation, with no one venturing beyond their borders."

Suddenly, something on the horizon caught Shaniah's attention. She squinted, unsure if the shimmering heat rising from the path was playing tricks on her vision. But no: there were definitely two figures approaching, their outlines becoming clearer with each passing moment.

"Wygia, look," she whispered, her hand instinctively moving to the hilt of her blade. "We're not alone after all."

As the figures drew nearer, Shaniah felt a surge of apprehension. The man and woman approaching were unlike anyone she had ever seen before. They stood taller than most, their height almost intimidating even from a distance. Shaniah found herself looking up at them as they came closer.

"Look at their proportions," said Wygia, fascinated. "They're similar to yours in some ways, but... different. Could they be...?"

"Full-blooded humans?" Shaniah finished, her voice barely above a whisper.

She couldn't recall what it was like to be in the presence of a full-blooded human. A realisation struck her like a physical blow: these strangers, with their height and unfamiliar proportions, were perhaps the closest she would ever come to seeing what her father might have looked like. For a moment, she lost herself in speculation, wondering if her father had been as tall, if his shoulders had been as broad, if his stride had been as confident.

"We should hope for the best, but prepare for the worst," Wygia murmured, her voice pulling Shaniah back to the present as she moved her hand to hover near her weapon. "We don't know if they're friendly or hostile."

Shaniah nodded, forcing herself to focus on the potential threat rather than her curiosity. As they continued down the path, drawing ever closer to the approaching pair, tension coiled in her muscles. Her hand remained poised over her sheath, ready to draw her blade at a moment's notice.

As both parties neared each other, the air grew thick with unspoken wariness. Shaniah found herself holding her breath, acutely aware of every movement, every subtle shift in posture that might signal aggression.

"Greetings, travellers," said the man, breaking the tense silence with a note of hesitant camaraderie. "I'm Turon, and this is my wife, Maril."

Shaniah studied them intently, taking in every detail. Turon was indeed tall, his frame solid and muscular beneath travel-worn clothing. His face was weathered, with lines that spoke of both laughter and hardship, and his eyes, a warm brown, held a glimmer of kindness despite their current wariness. His hair, a rich chestnut colour streaked with grey at the temples, was tied back in a practical knot.

Maril, standing close to her husband, was nearly as tall. Her build was lean and athletic, suggesting a life of physical activity. Her hair, a vibrant red that gleamed in the setting sun, was braided intricately, revealing a pretty face. Her green eyes were sharp and intelligent, constantly scanning their surroundings as if assessing potential threats.

Both humans carried weapons – Turon a broadsword strapped to his back, and Maril a pair of wickedly curved daggers at her hips. Their stances spoke of readiness, of people accustomed to defending themselves.

Having witnessed her fair share of unpleasantness from the elves who resented her back in Tunildia, Shaniah had a gut feeling that the couple was most likely not a threat. She raised her hand in friendly greeting, surprised by her own confidence.

"I'm Shaniah," she said. "And this is Wygia. We're travelling to Blackwing."

At the mention of Blackwing, something flickered in Turon and Maril's eyes – a mixture of surprise and what Shaniah thought might be pity.

"Blackwing?" Maril repeated, her voice softer than Shaniah had been expecting. "That's... an interesting choice of destination. We've just come from there ourselves. We won't be going back."

"May I ask why?" Wygia asked, astonishment in her tone.

Turon and Maril exchanged a glance, a world of unspoken communication passing between them.

"Blackwing is no longer the kingdom it once was," Turon answered, his voice heavy with regret and frustration. "Under Queen Selia's rule, it has become a place of oppression and fear. There's little opportunity for those who aren't in her inner circle, and even less hope for change."

"The queen rules with an iron fist," added Maril, her expression darkening. "There's poverty, division among the people. We couldn't bear to stay and watch our home crumble any longer. We're seeking a better life in another kingdom. We're heading in the direction of Mercada."

Shaniah felt as if the ground had dropped out

from beneath her feet. Although she had suspected that Blackwing might have been in decline under Queen Selia's rule, the travellers' words confirmed her worst fears. The truth felt horribly damning. She trembled slightly as she braced herself to ask a difficult question.

"What... what was Blackwing like before Queen Selia? Before she took the throne?"

"Ah, now that was a golden age," Turon said, a wistful smile tugging at his lips as he exhaled a deep sigh. "Under King Vygor and Queen Nheve, Blackwing was a place of prosperity and harmony. They ruled with wisdom and compassion."

"The king and queen were beloved by all," Maril confirmed, her eyes shining with remembered joy. "It was a time of great progress and hope."

Shaniah felt tears threatening to spill, a lump forming in her throat. She swallowed hard.

"King Vygor and Queen Nheve... they were my parents," she said, struggling to keep her voice steady. "They were killed when I was just a baby."

Turon and Maril stood in stunned silence, processing the shocking revelation. Then, with a gentleness that belied his imposing stature, Turon reached out and placed a comforting hand on Shaniah's shoulder.

"Your parents were the finest rulers Blackwing has ever known," he said, his voice thick with emotion. "Their loss was a tragedy that shook the entire kingdom."

Maril nodded, her expression brimming with sympathy.

"It's widely believed in Blackwing that Queen Selia was behind their deaths," she said cautiously, her voice softening as she noticed the increasing distress in Shaniah's expression. "She rallied a group of radical humans who opposed the union between a human king and an elven queen. It was a dark day for our kingdom when she seized power. I hope this information doesn't bring you too much pain, but I believe you deserve to know the truth."

Shaniah felt as if her heart might shatter. This revelation confirmed King Bartolm's suspicions about what had transpired. The pain of her parents' deaths flared up anew, but with it came a fierce determination and a burning desire to right the wrongs that had been done.

"Please," Shaniah said quietly, her voice laced with urgency, "would you consider setting up camp with us tonight? I... we have so much to discuss. Our interests align more than you might realise."

Turon and Maril exchanged another glance, a silent conversation passing between them. After a moment, Turon nodded.

"We would be honoured," he said, a tired smile warming his weathered features. "It seems we have much to learn from each other."

Chapter Eleven

The sun had dipped below the horizon hours ago, leaving the forest shrouded in shadows and starlight. Shaniah sat cross-legged on the soft earth, watching as Wygia deftly added the final touches to their tent, her movements graceful and efficient. A short distance away, Maril was engaged in setting up the tent that she and Turon would be sharing.

Shaniah couldn't help but marvel at the strange twists of fate that had brought them together. Less than a day ago, she and Wygia had been alone on their journey. Now, they found themselves in the company of two full-blooded humans who had known and loved Shaniah's parents.

The crackle of the newly kindled fire drew Shaniah's attention. She watched as Wygia and Maril settled around the growing flames.

Then, she pushed herself to her feet, brushing off her leggings before joining them.

As they sat in companionable silence, the rustling of undergrowth announced Turon's return. He emerged from the darkness, his muscular arms laden with freshly caught meat. Shaniah's eyes widened at the sight, her stomach growling in anticipation of a proper meal after days of travel rations.

"A wild boar," Turon announced, his deep voice tinged with satisfaction. "It should provide us with a hearty meal and enough leftovers for the road ahead."

"Turon has always been an exceptional hunter," Maril told Shaniah and Wygia as she looked proudly at her husband. "Back in Blackwing, our neighbours often relied on his skills to supplement their own catches."

"I hope old Cedric and his family will manage without us," Turon mused, his brow furrowing slightly as he sat down next to Maril and began preparing the meat for cooking. "He was never much of a hunter himself, always grateful for our shared bounty."

"And little Fenna next door – her mother's been ill this past year," said Maril, her expression a mixture of concern and resignation. "We often shared our catches with them too."

"Tell us more about Blackwing under Queen Selia's rule," said Wygia. "Is it true that the majority of people are unhappy?"

Turon and Maril exchanged a loaded glance.

"Unhappy would be an understatement," Turon answered, his voice heavy with suppressed anger. "Queen Selia rules with an iron fist, crushing any hint of dissent. People live in constant fear, never knowing when they might fall afoul of her ever-changing decrees."

"It's why we left," said Maril. "Many have tried to leave, but Queen Selia's grip on the kingdom is tight – few manage to escape her reach. I suppose we should count ourselves lucky."

A heavy silence fell over the group at the thought of this grim reality. Shaniah's heart ached for the people of Blackwing, for the kingdom that should have been her home but had been twisted into a place of distress and oppression.

"Which brings us to a pressing question," Turon said, his voice edged with concern as it cut through Shaniah's thoughts. "Why in the world are you two heading towards Blackwing? Especially you, Wygia. There are no elves left in the kingdom now. Queen Selia made sure of that. It's strictly a human realm under her rule."

Shaniah felt Wygia stiffen beside her.

"Perhaps that is validation that my magic will be effective against Queen Selia," Wygia replied, a hint of steel in her voice as she lifted her chin defiantly. "If she has driven all elves from Blackwing, it may be because she is intimidated by the power we wield."

Turon and Maril exchanged another meaningful look. Shaniah could almost see the pieces falling into place in their minds.

"You're not simply travelling to Blackwing, are you?" said Maril, her words careful and measured as she addressed Shaniah. "You want to reclaim your birthright, to take back the throne that is rightfully yours."

Shaniah's heart skipped a beat. Though she wasn't surprised by Maril's perceptiveness, the question had still hit her with unexpected force.

"Yes," she said simply, drawing courage from Wygia sitting beside her. "That is our intention."

The admission hung in the air, impactful and profound. Turon and Maril's expressions shifted from surprise to concern as they considered the implications of this revelation.

"It's a noble goal," Turon said reservedly, "but I fear you may be underestimating the challenges that lie ahead. Queen Selia's hold on power is absolute; her methods are ruthless. It would take a great amount of force to unseat her. The magic of just two elven types, no matter how impressive individually, most likely wouldn't be enough."

Shaniah's face flushed with shame. She looked down at her hands, fiddling with the hem of her sleeve as a familiar feeling of inadequacy washed over her.

"I..." she began, her voice faltering.

She swallowed hard, trying to steady the tremor in her throat. She slowly met Turon and Maril's expectant gazes. The intensity of their attention amplified her discomfort, but she forced herself to continue.

"As a half-breed, I've never been able to perform elven magic. I've tried, believe me, but... it simply isn't in me."

The admission hung heavily, the crackling of the fire the only sound in the sudden silence. Shaniah braced herself for the disappointment, the pity she had seen so many times before when people realised she lacked the magical abilities they expected of her.

"But that's impossible," Maril said, her voice soft with wonder. "When you were a baby, living in Blackwing before..."

She trailed off, pain flickering across her face at the memory of the tragedy that had followed.

"Shaniah," Turon said, picking up where his wife had left off, his deep voice gentle but insistent. "It was common knowledge throughout the kingdom that you showed signs of magical potential. During royal addresses, your parents would often hold you, and it was not unusual to see you demonstrating basic involuntary magical responses typical of an elven infant. The very presence of such magic was a sign of your heritage and the promise of greater abilities to come."

Shaniah felt as if the ground had dropped out from beneath her. She stared at Turon and Maril, her mind reeling as she struggled to process this earth-shattering revelation.

"I... what? But that's not... I don't remember..."

"You were very young," Maril said softly. "You were just a few months old when..."

She didn't need to finish the sentence. The tragedy that had befallen Shaniah's parents spoke for itself.

Shaniah's world tilted on its axis as the

implications of the disclosure crashed over her. All her life, she had felt lacking and incomplete, enduring sidelong glances, whispered comments, and outright taunts from the elves in Tunildia for her apparent lack of magical ability. To learn now that she had once possessed the very power she longed for was both staggering and painful.

Shaniah took a shaky breath, trying to centre herself amidst the whirlwind of emotions.

"If I did have magic once," she said, "I don't have it anymore. I've tried countless times to access even the smallest spark of ability, but there's nothing. Just... emptiness."

Wygia, who had been quiet during this exchange, leaned in close to Shaniah, her eyes shining with a fierce determination.

"But don't you see?" she said. "This changes everything. If you had magic once, there's hope that it might still be within you, dormant perhaps, but not gone entirely."

Shaniah wanted to believe Wygia's optimistic words, but years of disappointment had taught her to guard her heart against such hope. She shook her head, a sad smile tugging at the corners of her mouth.

"I appreciate the thought," she said, "but I think it's best we focus on the challenges we know we can face, rather than pinning our hopes on magic that simply may not be in me anymore."

A heavy silence descended upon the group, making the crackling of the fire seem unnaturally loud in the stillness. Turon and Maril exchanged a glance, their expressions a blend of sympathy and barely contained anger at the injustices wrought upon the young woman before them.

"Shaniah," Maril began, breaking the silence at last, her voice soft and full of compassion. "I wish there was something we could do to ease your pain. It's clear you've lost so much to Queen Selia's greed."

Turon nodded in agreement, his weathered face creased with concern.

"To have your birthright stolen, your heritage denied, and now to learn of the magic you once possessed..." he said. "It's a burden no one should have to bear."

"Thank you," Shaniah managed, touched by the genuine care these virtual strangers were showing her.

"It's not just Shaniah who has suffered, is it?" Wygia said, as if sensing the need to shift the focus from Shaniah's personal pain. "From what you've told us, it seems that Queen Selia's reign has brought nothing but misery to everyone in Blackwing."

Turon's expression darkened at this, his hands clenching into fists in his lap.

"You're right about that," he agreed, a growl of resentment in his voice. "Queen Selia's dictatorship has torn families apart; it has seen good people dragged from their homes and imprisoned in the dungeons. It has crushed the spirit of a once-proud kingdom."

"The taxes she imposes are crippling," added Maril, her expression a mask of sorrow and barely contained rage. "Families struggle to put food on the table while Queen Selia's coffers overflow. And anyone who dares to speak out..."

She trailed off, a shudder running through her body.

"Disappears," Turon finished grimly. "Never to be seen or heard from again."

As Turon and Maril continued recounting the atrocities committed under Queen Selia's rule, Shaniah felt a fire beginning to burn within her. The pain of her own losses, though still acute, started to merge with a rising sense of righteous anger on behalf of all those who had suffered under the usurper queen's reign.

"She must have made so many enemies," Shaniah mused, her tone taking on a steely edge. "Surely there are many in Blackwing who long for change, who remember the peace and prosperity of my parents' rule?"

"If the majority of people in Blackwing oppose Queen Selia and her reign of terror, perhaps they could be rallied," said Wygia. "A rebellion, sparked from within."

Rebellion: the idea lingered in the air, charged with possibility and danger in equal measure. Turon and Maril shared another look, communicating in a way that needed no words.

"It would be incredibly risky," Turon said warily. "Queen Selia's spies are everywhere. One wrong word to the wrong person could mean a death sentence."

Maril nodded, but there was a fire in her eyes that hadn't been there before.

"But if we were careful…" she said, "if we only approached those we knew we could trust…"

As the four of them huddled closer, their voices urgent, a plan began to take shape. They agreed that for Shaniah and Wygia to simply march into Blackwing and declare Shaniah's right to the throne would be suicide. Queen Selia's forces would crush them before they could rally any support.

Instead, a more subtle approach was needed. Turon and Maril, with their knowledge of Blackwing and its people, would return to the kingdom's outskirts. From there, moving cautiously and speaking only to those they could trust, they would begin to spread the word of Shaniah's existence and her intention to reclaim her rightful place on the throne.

"We'll have to be incredibly careful," Turon

emphasised gravely. "We'll stick to the fringes of the kingdom, never staying in one place for too long. If word of our actions were to reach Queen Selia's ears…"

"We know the risks," Maril interjected, reaching out to clasp her husband's hand. "But for the chance to see Blackwing freed from Queen Selia's tyranny, to see the rightful heir restored to the throne, it will be worth it."

"I'm not sure it's right of me to ask that you put yourselves in such danger," Shaniah protested, even though part of her was thrilled at the possibility their plan presented.

"You're not asking, Shaniah," Turon refuted, shaking his head firmly. "We're offering. The people of Blackwing have suffered for too long under Queen Selia's rule. They deserve to know there's hope for a better future."

"And that hope is you," Maril added, passionately addressing Shaniah. "We remember what Blackwing was like under your parents' rule: the prosperity, the harmony. If you're anything like them – and

I believe you are – you'll be the queen Blackwing needs to heal and thrive."

As the fire burned low and the night deepened around them, they continued to refine their plan. There were risks to be calculated, contingencies to be considered, but beneath it all ran a thread of purpose that had been missing before. In this clearing, under the canopy of stars, the first seeds of rebellion had been sown. And though the path ahead would be fraught with danger, there was hope.

Chapter Twelve

Sunlight filtered into the clearing through the canopy of ancient trees, bathing Shaniah and Wygia in a soft, dappled glow. They sat in tense silence, constantly scanning the treeline for any sign of movement. It had been several days since they had parted ways with Turon and Maril, and with each passing hour, the feeling of worry grew heavier.

Shaniah picked absently at a loose thread on her sleeve, her mind racing with possibilities, each more dire than the last. What if Turon and Maril had been discovered? What if they were languishing in some dark dungeon beneath Queen Selia's castle, or worse? Shuddering at the thought, she had to force herself to take a deep breath and steady her nerves.

Beside her, Wygia sat cross-legged, her silver hair shimmering in the light. Although her face was a mask of calm concentration, Shaniah could see the tension in her shoulders. They were both acutely aware of how much rested on Turon and Maril's success – and their safe return.

"They should have been back by now," Shaniah murmured, breaking the silence that had stretched between them. "What if something's gone wrong?"

"We mustn't lose hope," said Wygia. "Turon and Maril know the risks. They're cautious and clever. If anyone can navigate the dangers of Blackwing, it's them."

Shaniah nodded, trying to draw strength from Wygia's words. Nevertheless, the gnawing worry persisted, a constant companion in the long hours of waiting.

After what felt like an eternity, a new sound cut through the forest's ambience. Shaniah sat bolt upright, her hand instinctively moving to the hilt of her blade. Beside her, Wygia was already on her feet, her body rigid and ready for action.

The sound became clearer, revealing voices, low and urgent, accompanied by the steady clip-clop of horse hooves and the creak of wheels. Shaniah's heart leapt into her throat. Could it be...?

As if in response to Shaniah's lingering question, much to her relief, Turon and Maril emerged from the treeline, guiding a sturdy horse that pulled a simple cart with a few blankets inside.

"You're back!" she exclaimed, rushing forward to meet them, Wygia close on her heels. "We were so worried!"

Turon's weathered face broke into a broad grin as he brought the cart to a halt.

"It's good to see you too," he said. "We've got news: good news."

"The word has spread like wildfire through Blackwing," Maril said excitedly. "People are ready, Shaniah. They're ready to fight for you, to reclaim the kingdom from Queen Selia's tyranny."

As Turon and Maril recounted their

experiences in Blackwing – the whispered conversations, the secret meetings, the growing network of supporters – Shaniah felt a mixture of exhilaration and trepidation coursing through her. It was really happening. The rebellion was taking shape, becoming a reality.

"Anyway," said Turon. "We need to move quickly. Get in the cart, both of you."

Shaniah and Wygia clambered into the cart, while Turon and Maril repositioned themselves in the driver's seat. Then, the cart lurched into motion, the steady rhythm of the horse's hooves providing a backdrop to Shaniah's racing thoughts.

The journey along the dirt road stretched on, each moment thick with tension. The once-familiar sounds of the forest, usually comforting in their predictability, now felt ominous, as if the very trees knew the danger they were heading towards. Every rustle in the underbrush, every distant birdcall seemed to carry a warning. The air grew cooler as they travelled, the late afternoon sun casting long shadows that danced eerily across the path.

Shaniah couldn't shake the feeling that they were being watched, though she knew it was probably her nerves playing tricks on her. She stole a glance at Wygia, who sat silent and still beside her, her expression unreadable. The road ahead twisted and turned, leading them deeper into the unknown. Each bump felt like a jolt of reality against the steady rhythm of the horse's gait, reminding Shaniah of the peril that lay ahead.

"We'll be there soon," Maril said, turning to address Shaniah and Wygia with a nervous unease in her expression. "You'd better hide under the blankets. Don't come out until you hear Turon's hunting whistle."

As the muffled sounds of nature gave way to the bustle of town, Shaniah's heart pounded in her chest as she realised they must now be in Blackwing. From beneath the blankets, she strained to make sense of the cacophony of sounds around them – the murmur of voices, the clatter of hooves on cobblestones, the creaking of doors and shutters.

And then, almost imperceptibly at first, a new sound joined the chorus: footsteps, many footsteps, falling into rhythm with the cart's progress. Unable to resist, Shaniah carefully, oh so carefully, lifted a corner of the blanket, creating the tiniest of gaps through which to peer. What she saw took her breath away.

Surrounding the cart, growing in number with each passing moment, was an army of men and women of all ages. Some had weapons, while others were empty-handed, but all had sheer conviction etched on their faces. They moved with purpose, their gazes fixed on a distant point that Shaniah couldn't yet see.

As they travelled deeper into the heart of Blackwing, the crowd continued to swell. Shaniah's heart swelled with it, a mixture of pride, hope, and fear battling within her. These people were risking everything for her, for the promise of a better future. The feeling of responsibility that settled upon her was daunting, but not unwelcome.

Finally, after what seemed like hours, the cart came to a stop. Shaniah heard Turon's whistle, low and melodic. Carefully, she and Wygia emerged from their hiding place, blinking rapidly in the fading light of day as they sat up and discarded their blankets.

They found themselves in a secluded spot behind what could only be Blackwing's castle, its imposing towers looming above them and the gathered crowd. Turon and Maril jumped down from the cart and turned to address the assembled rebels.

"Friends," Turon began, his voice quiet but assertive, capturing the attention of everyone present, "the time has come. We stand on the brink of a new era for Blackwing. But to bring about that change, we must first remove the tyrant who has undermined and oppressed our kingdom for far too long."

"Our plan is simple, but dangerous," Maril said firmly. "We storm the castle, fighting our way to the throne room where Queen Selia undoubtedly hides. From there, we put an end to her reign of terror once and for all."

A murmur of anticipation ran through the crowd. Shaniah felt her stomach clench at the finality of Maril's words. This was it. There was no turning back now.

"Your magic may well prove to be the deciding factor in this fight," Turon said, turning to address Wygia. "Queen Selia has no defence against it. When the moment comes, do not hesitate."

"I understand," Wygia said earnestly. "I will do whatever is necessary to see Shaniah take her rightful place on the throne."

As the rebels began to organise themselves, preparing for the assault on the castle, Shaniah sat rooted to the spot, her mind reeling. Her entire life had been leading up to this moment, but now that it was finally here, she felt a flicker of doubt. Was she truly ready for this?

When she looked around at the determined faces of those who had rallied to her cause, it sparked a sudden surge of resolve. These people believed in her and in the future she represented. She couldn't let them down. It was now or never.

Chapter Thirteen

The rebels stormed through the castle gardens, their boots trampling the carefully manicured paths as they raced towards the imposing stone walls. The scent of crushed flowers mingled with the sharp tang of sweat and fear in the air. Shaniah and Wygia followed close behind, their hearts pounding in unison with the battle cries that filled the night.

Reaching the castle itself, several particularly burly folk at the front of the crowd battered down the entrance, the ancient doors giving way under the relentless assault. The rebels then surged into the castle's interior, the sound of their entry reverberating through the stone corridors as they pressed on.

Guards emerged from every shadow, their faces a picture of alarm as they beheld the sheer number of insurgents. Steel clashed against steel, the cacophony of combat reverberating all around. Shaniah found herself swept up in the chaos, her blade singing as she parried and struck, defending those around her with a ferocity that surprised even herself.

Wygia was a whirlwind of elven grace, her magic crackling through the air like lightning. With each gesture of her hands, guards were thrown back, their weapons clattering uselessly to the ground.

As the rebels pushed deeper into the castle, Shaniah's attention was suddenly caught by a flicker of movement above. She paled in shock at the sight before her: ravens – dozens of them, perched on ornate sconces and lurking in the shadowy recesses of the vaulted ceilings. Their obsidian eyes seemed to follow her every move, silent witnesses to the upheaval unfolding beneath them.

The significance was not lost on her. It was as if some force beyond this realm had been guiding her, nudging her along a path she couldn't quite see. All those raven sightings: they must have been pointing to a purpose far greater than herself. And now, that purpose was right in front of her. This feeling of destiny, of being part of a larger plan, gave her both comfort and unease.

Finally, after what seemed like an eternity of fighting, the rebels reached the large double doors of the throne room. Turon and Maril threw their weight against them, causing the ornate wood to give way with a resounding crack.

As they spilled into the cavernous chamber, Shaniah's breath caught in her throat. The throne room was awash with even more ravens, their black feathers a stark contrast against the opulent gold and crimson décor. They perched on every available surface, their silence adding to the surreal atmosphere.

Beyond the ravens, it was the figure on the throne that captured Shaniah's attention. Queen Selia sat rigid, her knuckles white as she gripped the armrests of her ill-gotten seat of power. The usurper was a study in contrasts: with high cheekbones, full lips, and eyes the colour of storm clouds, her beauty was undeniable, but there was a hardness to her features, a cruelty etched into the lines around her mouth. Her gown was a masterpiece of elegance: midnight blue silk embroidered with silver thread that caught the light during every subtle movement. A crown of black iron sat heavily upon her long dark hair, its jagged peaks reminiscent of the very ravens that filled the room.

An intense wave of emotions crashed over Shaniah, threatening to engulf her. The woman before her was the one responsible for having torn her family apart, the one who had robbed her of her parents. Hatred surged through Shaniah's veins, mingling with a grief she had long tried to bury. She had imagined this moment so many times, envisioned how it would feel to finally face the woman who had caused her so much pain. Nothing could have prepared her for the reality of seeing Queen Selia, so close, so tangible, the architect of her nightmares in the flesh.

As more rebels flooded into the chamber, Shaniah saw a glint of fear flicker across Queen Selia's face, only to be quickly masked by a sneer of contempt. However, the panic in her eyes betrayed her, revealing the depth of her realisation that she was hopelessly outnumbered.

Shaniah stepped forward, despite the tumult of emotions roiling within her.

"Queen Selia," she said boldly, the title feeling like a curse on her tongue, "your reign of terror ends today. I am Shaniah, daughter of King Vygor and Queen Nheve. I have come to reclaim what you stole from me – and from all of Blackwing."

Queen Selia's face paled in horror, her composure cracking as she beheld the living embodiment of her greatest crime.

"Impossible," she said with a bitter snarl, her voice dripping with venom even as fright made it quiver. "You can't be… I made sure…"

"You made sure of what?" Shaniah pressed, taking another step closer to the throne. "That my parents were dead? That their infant daughter would never return to challenge your rule?"

"I did no such thing," Queen Selia said feebly, her eyes darting between Shaniah and the armed rebels. "Your parents' deaths were a tragedy, but I had no part in them."

A murmur of anger rippled through the crowd. Turon stepped forward, his face twisted with rage.

"Enough of your lies!" he roared. "We all know the truth. Confess your crimes, or face the wrath of those you've oppressed for so long."

Surrounded by a sea of hostile faces and weapons glinting with the promise of violence, Queen Selia's façade began to crack. Her breath quickened as she searched desperately for an escape, but there wasn't one. The room seemed to close in on her, the weight of the rebels' fury pressing down like an iron vice. She trembled slightly, but still tried to maintain her composure.

"You're all fools," she countered angrily, pushing herself from her throne, though her voice wavered as she stood. "Do you think you can scare me into confessing? I've survived worse than this. I've held this throne through sheer will. I..."

Her words faltered as she met Shaniah's gaze, the depth of hatred in her challenger's eyes more terrifying than any weapon. The silence in the chamber was thick and oppressive, as if the very air was waiting for the tyrant to break. Her bravado continued to slip as she realised that the rebels weren't just angry: they were ready to kill her.

"Fine!" she finally blurted, desperation lacing her voice. "Yes, I had them killed. They were weak, too soft to rule. I did what was necessary!"

A roar of outrage erupted from the rebels, but Shaniah barely heard it. A strange sensation began to build within her, starting at her core and radiating out to her fingertips. It was as if her very blood was singing, pulsing with an energy she had never felt before. The anger she had carried for so long – at the loss of her parents, at the years of doubt and insecurity, at the suffering inflicted on the people of Blackwing – reached a crescendo.

Her vision narrowed, the throne room fading away until all she could see was Queen Selia's face. In that moment, Shaniah felt something snap inside, destroying the last of her restraint. It was as if a dam had broken, releasing something raw and primal.

Almost without conscious thought, Shaniah thrust her hands forward. Time seemed to slow as she watched her fingers spread wide, her palms facing the woman who had stolen everything from her. For a heartbeat, nothing happened. Then, with a thunderous crash, a surge of fire erupted from her palms.

The living torrent of flames seemed to possess a will of its own. It raced forward, immediately crossing the distance between Shaniah and Queen Selia, its colours shifting from deep crimson to blinding white, veined with electric blue tendrils that crackled with power.

The inferno engulfed Queen Selia in an instant, wrapping around her like a ravenous beast finally claiming its long-awaited prey. The tyrant's eyes widened in panic, her terrified screams instantly swallowed by the ear-shattering sound of the flames. The fire clung to her form, moulding itself to every contour of her body, a deadly embrace from which there was no escape. She raised her arms in a futile attempt to ward off the inevitable, her fingers splaying as if she could push back the tide of flames through sheer force of mind.

The magical fire consumed the tyrant with a voracity that defied all natural laws. It burned hotter and faster than any mundane flame, its hunger insatiable. Her flesh blackened and crumbled, her bones igniting like kindling, cracking and splintering under the immense heat. The outline of her face, contorted in a plea of agony, became a haunting vision.

The crown, once a symbol of her ill-gotten power, met a fate as dramatic as its wearer. The black iron began to glow, first a dull red, then brightening to orange, yellow, and finally a blinding white. It softened and lost its shape, the jagged peaks drooping and melding together. Within a matter of heartbeats, the crown was reduced to a puddle of molten metal, hissing and spitting as it pooled on the throne room floor. The liquefied metal then bubbled violently, vapour rising in great plumes as it disintegrated.

Everyone watched in awe and revulsion as the spectacle unfolded. The ravens flew around in panic, a swirling mass of black feathers. Their harsh cries added to the cacophony of the firestorm.

As the flames consumed the last vestiges of Queen Selia, they began to coalesce, swirling inwards like a tornado in reverse. They spun faster and faster, compressing into a blindingly bright sphere that hovered in the air where the woman had stood just moments before. For a breathless second, the sphere pulsed there, a miniature sun born of vengeance and long-dormant magic.

Then, with a sound like a thunderclap, the sphere imploded, collapsing in on itself and vanishing in a dazzling flash of light that left afterimages dancing in the eyes of everyone present.

A silence fell over the throne room, broken only by the soft patter of ash settling on the polished floor – all that remained of Queen Selia, the woman who had stolen a kingdom and orphaned a princess.

Chapter Fourteen

Shaniah remained frozen in the aftermath of her explosive display of power, her eyes fixed on the spot where Queen Selia had stood just moments before. The air still crackled with residual energy, and the acrid scent of smoke hung heavy in the large throne room. Her hands, which had unleashed such devastating magic, trembled at her sides. Her mind reeled as she tried to comprehend what had just transpired.

When Turon and Maril had spoken of the potential she'd shown as a baby, Shaniah had truly believed that part of her had died long ago and could never be rekindled. But now, as she stood amidst the stunned silence of everyone around her, she grappled with the occurrence that had just shattered everything she had ever believed about herself. The magic that had erupted from her was undeniable, its power raw and palpable. The shame of her perceived deficiency, an ache that had been a constant companion throughout her life, had now vanished completely.

As the shock began to ebb, giving way to a maelstrom of confusion and wonder, Shaniah felt a gentle touch on her arm. She turned to see Wygia, whose expression was a profound blend of awe and understanding.

"Shaniah," she said, "what we just witnessed... it was extraordinary. Your magic... it's been there all along, waiting to be awakened."

"But how? I've never... I thought I was..."

"I believe your fury at Queen Selia, the culmination of years of pain and loss, must have broken through whatever barriers were holding your magic at bay," said Wygia, giving Shaniah's arm a passionate squeeze. "Think about it: You grew up believing yourself an orphan, yearning for parents you didn't even remember. That kind of deep-seated pain, that longing... it could have suppressed your innate magical abilities, keeping them dormant until this very moment."

As Wygia's words sank in, Turon and Maril came over to Shaniah, their faces etched with amazement and pride.

"Wygia's theory makes sense," Turon said. "Trauma, especially in young children, can lead to all kinds of unexpected outcomes."

"Indeed," Maril agreed, her eyes shimmering with unshed tears. "You've been through so much, Shaniah. I think I speak for all of us when I say that we're immensely proud of you."

Taking a deep breath to steady herself, Shaniah looked around the throne room, taking in the sheer number of people who had fought alongside her, who had risked everything for this moment. As she observed the fascination and expectation on their faces, the enormity of what had just happened – and what was yet to come – settled upon her.

"So what now?" she asked, her voice tinged with uncertainty. "Do you all want me to take the throne, just like that?"

The room fell into a contemplative silence as

Shaniah's question hung in the air. Then gradually, the crowd, still processing the intensity of Queen Selia's demise after decades of tyranny, began to exchange glances and murmurs of relief.

"Yes," Turon said firmly, his voice steady despite the emotion of the moment. "We've seen what you're capable of. You've shown us your strength and resolve. We believe you're the one who can lead us forward."

"We've all seen the courage you've displayed," said Maril. "Your actions have proved you're more than ready to take on this role. We want you to lead us, to restore Blackwing to what it should be."

"You've earned this," said an older man in the crowd. "You're our hope for the future."

One by one, everyone expressed their support, their voices rising in a chorus of affirmations. As Shaniah looked around the room, still trying to take it all in, her focus settled on a group of ravens perched on a high ledge. These birds, and their appearances at pivotal moments in her life, must have been guiding her towards this very day.

"What about all these ravens?" she asked, her voice tinged with wonder and a hint of trepidation. "Do they want me here in this castle that they have clearly occupied for so long?"

As if in response to Shaniah's question, a sleek black raven detached itself from its perch and glided gracefully towards her. With a gentle flutter of its wings, it alighted on her shoulder, its obsidian eyes meeting hers with an intelligence that seemed far beyond that of an ordinary bird.

Though the raven made no sound, Shaniah felt a connection, a wordless communication that resonated deep within her. In that moment, she understood with perfect clarity that the ravens not only accepted her presence, but welcomed it. They had been waiting, just as she had been, for this day to come.

A profound sense of relief washed over Shaniah. It was accompanied by a feeling of completion she had never experienced before. The ravens she had encountered throughout her life had not been mere coincidences or random sightings. They had been harbingers, silent messengers trying to guide her towards her destiny. And now, that destiny had finally come to fruition.

As she stood there with the raven perched regally on her shoulder and with the admiring gaze of the crowd fixed upon her, Shaniah made a decision. The knowledge of her lifelong connection to these mysterious birds would remain her secret – a private understanding between herself and the winged creatures that had watched over her journey.

With a newfound sense of purpose and belonging, Shaniah straightened her posture and lifted her chin. The throne of Blackwing awaited its rightful ruler, and she was finally ready to claim it. In that moment, as the weight of her new responsibilities settled upon her, she realised that her life had been leading to this very point all along. She was no longer just Shaniah, the half-breed orphan who believed herself to be without magic. She was Queen Shaniah Blackwing, destined ruler of a kingdom on the brink of a new era.

Epilogue

With Queen Selia's tyrannical reign finally over, Shaniah wasted no time in setting things right in the kingdom of Blackwing. She made it her first priority to ensure that everyone had enough to eat, redistributing wealth and resources to those who had been deprived for so long. The dungeons, once filled with the wails of the unjustly imprisoned, were emptied, their inhabitants freed from the torturous conditions that had been their daily reality. Shaniah made it her mission to banish fear from her kingdom, to create a land where no one would ever again have to live under the shadow of dread. With the help of Wygia, Turon, Maril, and every loyal subject, the word spread quickly, and Blackwing began to heal.

In recognition of their bravery and leadership, Shaniah appointed Turon and

Maril as honorary members of her royal council. Their wisdom and courage would help guide the kingdom into its new era of prosperity.

Having put Blackwing back on the right path, Shaniah and Wygia returned to Tunildia. The first order of business was to deliver the news to King Bartolm. Upon hearing that Queen Selia's reign of terror had ended and that Shaniah had avenged the deaths of King Vygor and Queen Nheve, a weight seemed to lift from King Bartolm's shoulders. Though nothing could ever bring his sister and her husband back, the knowledge that justice had been served gave him a sense of peace that had long eluded him.

While in Tunildia, Shaniah made sure to express her heartfelt gratitude to King Bartolm and Kimdah. Their love and guidance had shaped her into the woman she had become. Shaniah and Wygia also thanked Commander Broman Cillidah and his army for having prepared them so well for their quest to Blackwing.

The elves of Tunildia who had once looked down on Shaniah for being a half-breed now treated her with a newfound respect. Her bravery in having brought down an evil queen had earned her their admiration, and even the most outspoken sceptics – Kei included – could no longer deny her worth.

Wygia remained in Tunildia to fulfil her duties as a princess, but she and Shaniah knew their bond would keep the connection between the two kingdoms strong. They planned to meet frequently, ensuring that the ties between Blackwing and Tunildia would only grow stronger with time.

Now that Shaniah knew she possessed magic, ironically, she wasn't too concerned with using it. Despite how badly she had once yearned for such power, she realised she didn't need to rely on it. The strength she had developed throughout her life without it was more than enough. The magic was there, should she ever need it, but it wouldn't define her.

Soon feeling at ease with her new role and her new home in Blackwing's castle, Shaniah happily shared her living quarters with the ravens that had been her silent guides. Though she kept the true nature of their influence a secret, she found comfort in their presence, knowing they had played a significant role in her journey.

No longer were elves banned from Blackwing; instead, they were welcomed. The kingdom thrived as a place of unity and acceptance. As a half-breed, Shaniah had swiftly ended the old prejudices perpetuated by the evil queen, paving the way for a brighter future.

For the first time in her life, Shaniah felt at peace, and for many others, there was now hope.